Regina Public Library
BOOK SALE ITEM
Non-returnable

Dear Parents and Educators,

Welcome to Penguin Young Readers! As parents and educators, you know that each child develops at his or her own pace—in terms of speech, critical thinking, and, of course, reading. Penguin Young Readers recognizes this fact. As a result, each Penguin Young Readers book is assigned a traditional easy-to-read level (1–4) as well as a Guided Reading Level (A–P). Both of these systems will help you choose the right book for your child. Please refer to the back of each book for specific leveling information. Penguin Young Readers features esteemed authors and illustrators, stories about favorite characters, fascinating nonfiction, and more!

Ella the Elephant™: Ella's School Picture Day

LEVEL 2
GUIDED READING LEVEL H

This book is perfect for a **Progressing Reader** who:

- can figure out unknown words by using picture and context clues;
- can recognize beginning, middle, and ending sounds;
- can make and confirm predictions about what will happen in the text; and
- can distinguish between fiction and nonfiction.

Here are some **activities** you can do during and after reading this book:

- Make Connections: In this story, Ella and her friends try new looks for Picture Day. What would you wear for your Picture Day? Draw a picture of your outfit and write a sentence or two describing what you are wearing.
- Sight Words: Sight words are frequently used words that readers must know just by looking at them. They are known instantly, on sight. Knowing these words helps children develop into efficient readers. As you read the story, have the child point out the sight words below.

after	had	going	pretty	thank
any	her	just	take	walk

Remember, sharing the love of reading with a child is the best gift you can give!

—Bonnie Bader, EdM
Penguin Young Readers program

*Penguin Young Readers are leveled by independent reviewers applying the standards developed [illegible] and Gay Su Pinnell in *Matching Books to Readers: Using Leveled Books in Guided Reading*, Heinemann, 1999.

PENGUIN YOUNG READERS
An Imprint of Penguin Random House LLC

Based on "Stylish Ella" from the animated television series *Ella the Elephant.* Story by Sheila Dinsmore. Teleplay by Ben Joseph. ELLA THE ELEPHANT™ and all related logos and characters are trademarks of DHX Cookie Jar Inc. Ella the Elephant © 2013 CJ Ella Productions. Inc. DHX MEDIA ® DHX Media Ltd.

Penguin supports copyright. Copyright fuels creativity, encourages diverse voices, promotes free speech, and creates a vibrant culture. Thank you for buying an authorized edition of this book and for complying with copyright laws by not reproducing, scanning, or distributing any part of it in any form without permission. You are supporting writers and allowing Penguin to continue to publish books for every reader.

© 2015 DHX Cookie Jar Inc. Book adapted by Lana Jacobs. Published by Penguin Young Readers, an imprint of Penguin Random House LLC, 345 Hudson Street, New York, New York 10014.
Printed in the USA.

ISBN 978-0-448-48922-3 10 9 8 7 6 5 4 3 2 1

Ella's School Picture Day

Penguin Young Readers
An Imprint of Penguin Random House

Ella the Elephant is at school.

She paints pictures

with her friends.

What fun!

Tiki thinks about what to paint.

Frankie paints a picture,

and his hands.

The paint must come off

his hands soon.

Tomorrow is Picture Day!

Belinda loves Picture Day.

She likes to smile for pictures.

Ella loves Picture Day, too.

She likes to be in pictures.

After school, Belinda has an idea.

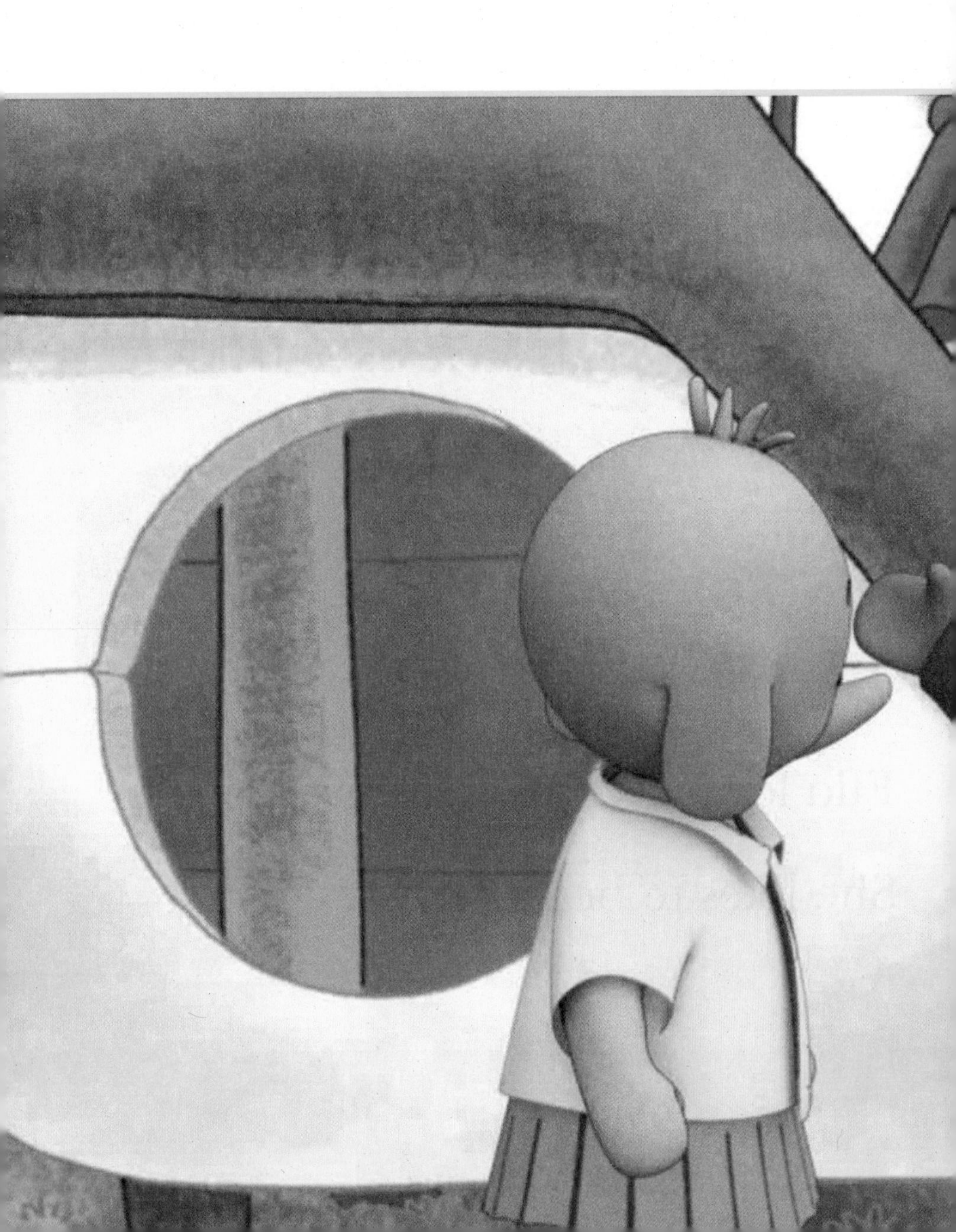

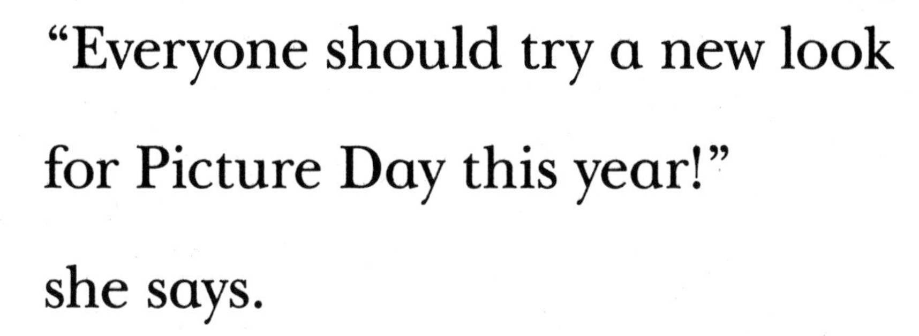

"Everyone should try a new look

for Picture Day this year!"

she says.

Belinda tells Tiki she should not wear her glasses.

Tiki says she can try that.

“I’m going to bring a new purse for Picture Day,” says Belinda.

What will Ella do for Picture Day?

Belinda has an idea!

"You should wear

a pretty new hat,"

says Belinda.

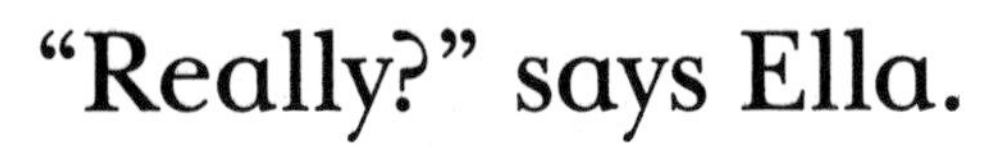

"Really?" says Ella.

"But I like my magic red hat."

Belinda and Ella go shopping.

They see a lot of hats.

Belinda thinks they are all beautiful!

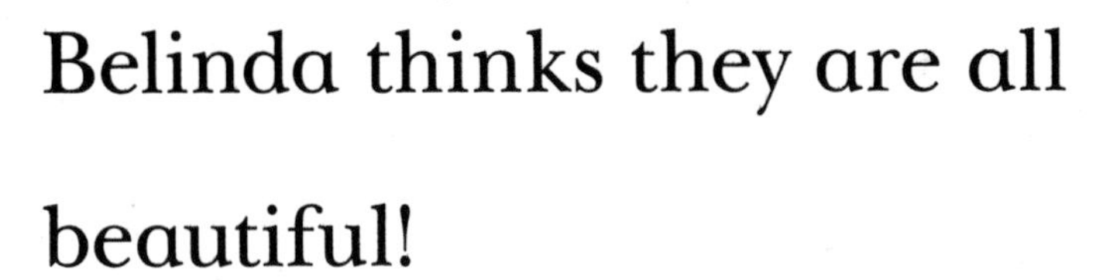

But Ella is not so sure.

Ella does not like any of the hats.

Wait!

Belinda finds a hat

she thinks is just right for Ella.

Ella shows Tiki her new hat.

“The feathers are soft,” says Tiki.

“Belinda says they are pretty,” says Ella.

Ella and Frankie play a game together in the park.

Uh-oh!

Ella cannot see very well

with her new hat on.

The feathers get in her way.

At the park, Ella and her friends read books.

Uh-oh!

A bird thinks Ella's hat

is a nest!

Ella goes home.

She tries to help her mom

bake a cake.

“Is something wrong, Ella?”

asks Ella’s mom.

"I'm too hot!" says Ella.

The feathers on her hat

are making her very hot.

Finally, Picture Day is here.

Ella and her friends

walk to school together.

Belinda has a new purse.

Ella is wearing her new hat.

Tiki is not wearing her glasses.

Tiki bumps into Belinda.

Belinda's new purse goes flying!

"Uh-oh!" says Belinda.

Her purse is on the lamppost.

Belinda needs help

to get her purse back.

Ella wants to help.

But her new hat

can't help fix the problem.

Her new hat is not a magic hat.

Ella goes home

to get her magic hat.

Ella comes back

with her magic hat.

She has an idea.

“Magic hat, here we go!”

Ella says.

Ella's magic hat turns into a boomerang.

The boomerang knocks Belinda's purse down from the lamppost.

"Thank you, Ella!" Belinda says.

"Now I'm ready for Picture Day!"

At school, Mrs. Briggs takes pictures of Ella and her friends. "Let's take one of us all together!" says Ella. "Hooray for Picture Day!" says Belinda.